Do I Have To Take Violet?

Do I Have To

SUÇIE STEVENSON

Take Violet?

A PICTURE YEARLING BOOK

FOR POP

Published by
Dell Publishing
a division of
Bantam Doubleday Dell Publishing Group, Inc.
666 Fifth Avenue
New York, New York 10103

ISBN: 0-440-40682-X

Reprinted by arrangement with The Putnam & Grosset Book Group

Printed in the United States of America
August 1992
10 9 8 7 6 5 4 3 2 1

"Mercy! That banging!" said Mama. "That clanging!
    All from one small child."
"Spoon-a-looney…spooney-tooney," sang Violet loudly.
"I can't hear myself think," sighed Mama.

"Spoon-a-looney…spooney-tooney," sang Violet even louder.
"Must you sing that song, Violet? Where on earth is Elly
    when I need her?"

"Thank goodness! There you are Elly."
"I was just going to ride my bike," said Elly, "BY MYSELF."

"…spooney-tooney….Can I come too?" asked Violet.

"Forget it," Elly answered.

"Be a dear, Elly, and take your sister out for a walk."

"Do I *have* to take Violet?" Elly moaned.

"Please, Elly, I need some peace and quiet," said Mama.

"*She* needs peace and quiet, what about me? Good work,
    Violet, now I'm stuck with you again," Elly grumbled.
    "I could go swimming, but not with you.
    I could climb way up high in a tree, but not with you.
    I could skateboard really fast, but not with you.
    I can't have any fun with a baby like you!"

"But since I've got you, let's go down to the rocks."
"Oh boy!" exclaimed Violet.
The two sisters started off across the lawn and headed
  for the rocky beach.

"Going to the rocksies-boxsies-tocky-yocksies," sang Violet.
"Shh!" said Elly. "We don't want to wake the sleeping dragons."

"Dragons?" asked Violet, in a whisper.
"Millions of them," said Elly. "We have to sneak past them
    to get to the rocks. Didn't I tell you? I've seen red ones
    and pink ones, and green ones and orange ones.
    Every color. Especially…"

"...the yellow SNAPDRAGONS. ROARR!" shouted Elly.
    "Watch this, Violet." Elly made their petals open and close.
"Hah!" said Violet, "they have fuzzy yellow tongues!
    These dragons aren't scary at all."

The girls climbed down onto the warm rocks by the sea.
"Rocks and snails…rocks and snails…" sang Violet.
"Violet! Don't bother me. And no singing!"

Elly tried to nap, when she felt something crawling under
her leg. Elly's eyes popped open. "*What* are you doing?"
she demanded.
"Getting a rock," answered Violet.
"What's wrong with the rocks over there?"
"I need this blue one. You're sitting on all
the good rocks," said Violet.

Elly shut her eyes again. Violet continued to collect rocks,
and quietly decorated Elly with them. Then she watched
Elly sleep for awhile…until she couldn't wait any longer.
"When are you going to wake up?" yelled Violet,
as she wiggled her finger in Elly's ear.

"Violet! You are such a nuisance!"

The two sisters sat on a rock, watching the waves roll
in and out...and in and out....Finally, Elly asked,
"Did you ever see a monster, Violet?
Sometimes they live near rocks like these."

"Are they big?" asked Violet.
"Pretty big," said Elly, "and slimy."
"Do you see any monsters now?" asked Violet.
"Not yet," said Elly. "You stay here,
    and I'll go look around."

Violet sniffed the salty air. She stared at the waves
and the passing boats, and kept her feet tucked in.

Suddenly she heard an awful groan. Then CRACK…
GURGLE, GURGLE. Horrible slippery, slimy
arms wrapped around Violet.
"Help, Elly! Come quick! Save me,
it's the monsters!" screamed Violet.

"Ha, ha! Scared you. And it serves you right!" said Elly,
as she jumped up from behind the rock where
Violet was sitting.
"You're a meany!" said Violet. "That's not fair!"

"I want to go home," said Violet.
"We can't go home yet," said Elly.
"I'm going home now," said Violet.
"Good, go home, fine with me," said Elly.
Violet wandered off by herself.

Elly grew bored with staring at the ocean and she began to miss her sister. "Oh, Violet!" Elly called, "I was only joking." Elly leapt from rock to rock, searching for Violet. Looking down, she saw a long black snake slithering across the rocks.

"YIPES! SNAKES! GET ME OUT OF HERE!" screamed Elly.

"Hah!" said Violet, waving a stick. "Scared YOU!
    Serves YOU right!"
"Very funny, Violet," muttered Elly.

"I see I'm going to have to keep my eye on you," said Elly
to her sister. Violet pressed her nose against Elly's.
"We better do something that's fun together."
"Like what?" asked Violet.

"Well…let's see….Here's a nice flat rock," said Elly.
"It will make a good table. Let's have a banquet."
"A what?" asked Violet.
"A big fancy supper party," Elly answered. "We'll find
    everything for our table right here on these rocks.
    First, you clean those snails off the table.
    I'll go look for dishes."

Before long Elly came back carrying big white clam shells.
"These will do quite nicely for dishes," she said.
But Violet was too busy to even notice. She was arranging
    the snails on the big rock. "Some for me and some for you,"
    sang Violet, "some for me and some for you, some for…."
"Violet! Don't sort them, just get rid of them!" yelled Elly.

Violet quickly swept the snails off the rock.
"That's enough!" cried Elly.

"What could we serve in these clam shells, Violet?"
"Soup!" answered Violet.
"But what kind of soup?"
"Seaweed soup."
"Good idea, Violet. Here's some seaweed."
Elly gave Violet a slimy pile.

"Soup is fun," said Violet, as she tore up
the seaweed into lots of little pieces.

"Now," said Elly, "we've got the vegetable for our soup,
  but what about the broth?" She thought for awhile
  and then said, "Violet, take this shell. I'll hold you…
  like this, and you scoop up some sea water.
  Just be careful to do it fast…because here comes…"

"…a wave."

The sisters dried off in the sun while collecting things
for their table.

"Look, Violet, this seaweed has bubbles in it that you
can pop like firecrackers. Let's use them for party favors."
"I like this part best," said Violet.
"Don't pop them all now," said Elly.

The girls set the table with shells and sticks and colored
   pebbles, snails, blue mussels, and sea lavender.
Then they got all dressed up for their fancy supper.
"My dear," said Elly, "your hair looks just lovely today.
   Are those crab earrings?"

"And you have such beautiful feathers in your hair,"
said Violet. "I wish I had a feather too."
Elly gave her one.

The girls stirred their seaweed soup with sticks.
"Everything is just perfect, except for one thing,"
    moaned Elly. "We can't eat any of this stuff."
"I'm hungry," said Violet.
"I'm starving," said Elly.

"Lunchtime!" they heard their mother call.
"Yippie!" said Elly.
"Oh boy!" said Violet.
The girls jumped up and ran to meet their mother.
"Can we eat sandwiches?" asked Violet.
"Certainly," said Mama, as she lifted them
    up over the seawall.
"Sandwiches-banwiches-can-canwiches!"
    sang Violet and Elly together.

The sisters walked back to the house.
"Elly, will you go down to the rocks again, sometime?"
    asked Violet.
"Sure, I might…but not without you," said Elly.
    "Who would make the soup?"